WINTER WEDDING

Rochelle Paige

Crystal,
    The dedication doesn't even begin to describe what your friendship means to me.

♡ Ro

COPYRIGHT

©2014 Rochelle Paige Popovic

All rights reserved.

Edited by Mickey Reed

Cover designed by Melissa Gill

Crystal,
The dedication doesn't even begin to describe what your friendship means to me.
RP ♥

DEDICATION

Crystal-

My publishing journey with the Blythe College series started with you letting me know in the middle of the night that Push the Envelope went live. While I had fallen asleep on my couch waiting on Amazon, you persisted in your stalking of them until it went live. You've cracked me up on FaceTime while we learned about author takeovers together, hammered out plot points with me, inspired me with your books, and invited me into your life and home. I couldn't let this series end without telling you how very much your friendship means to me. Love you, girl!

PROLOGUE

Alexa

"Yes!" I shrieked as I threw myself off the bed and into Drake's arms in response to his proposal. "A million times yes."

Knowing he'd been holding on to an engagement ring for so many months was a shock, although a much more pleasant one than the other one I'd received tonight. Sure, the idea of marrying Drake had crossed my mind from time to time even though our relationship was still relatively new and we were young. I'd been hiding after what had happened with Brad. His betrayal had made me lose faith in boys and love. Meeting Drake had brought me back to life and made me want more again, but we still had another year of school until we graduated from college. As much as I could picture myself with him forever, I hadn't expected us to be engaged this soon.

Even though the timing wasn't perfect and tonight was terrifyingly insane, there was no other answer I could give. The bottom line was this: I loved Drake beyond distraction and wanted to spend the rest of my life with him.

"You know you're crazy, right?" I asked as I stared at the ring he had slid on my finger.

Drake flashed a grin my way, the one that showed off the dimple in his left cheek. "Crazy in love with you."

1

My panties practically melted at his answer. "Your kind of crazy must be contagious then because I love you more than I ever expected it was possible to love another person."

"How about you show me just how crazy we can be together?" he breathed out as his lips trailed down my neck.

I pushed him onto his back on the carpeted floor and tore my sleep shirt over my head. By the time the fabric hit the floor, he'd managed to strip off all his clothes. His hand was stroking lightly his hardened cock as he watched me slide my pajama pants off. I licked my lips at the sight, desperate to taste him.

"You're so fucking beautiful, baby," he murmured softly, his love shining brightly from his lust-darkened gaze.

Leaning over to lick the drop of pre-come glistening on his tip, I heard him groan. His hands tangled in my hair, but they pulled me away instead of closer to his erection.

"Drake, please," I begged, desperate to taste him.

"Oh, you'll get it. Don't worry about that. I want those pretty lips wrapped around me, but I want you to do it with my face buried between your legs," he said before swallowing hard. "I want you to feel with every throb of my cock how fucking hot it makes me when I devour your pussy. Now slide your ass up here and give me what I want."

I crawled alongside him and kissed him deeply before turning around. Placing my knees on either side of his shoulders, I straddled his face. His breath was hot against my naked flesh as his tongue flicked out for a quick lick.

"Lower," he rasped before he grabbed my hips and yanked me onto his lips.

I pitched forward at the shock of sensation, suddenly on the edge of a climax before he'd even had the chance to do much of anything. Determination filled me. I wanted to drive him insane

2

before I let myself go. Leaning forward, I sucked his straining cock into my mouth and swirled my tongue over the head. His groan caused a vibration, and I felt my walls clench on his tongue as his cock pulsed in my mouth.

My cheeks hollowed out as I sucked hard, bobbing up and down on his length in a frenzy. His hips surged in rhythm with my movements and his tongue lapped at me as he held my hips tight so I couldn't wiggle away. Not that I wanted to get away from him. Even as he grew harder and thicker in my mouth, his cock nudging against my throat, I felt myself lose control. He moaned again, and this time, it was enough to send me flying over the edge. As I shuddered from the sheer force of my climax, my legs shook as I held on to his thighs while I came.

When Drake pulled out of my mouth, I tried to protest, but no words would form yet. Pushing me lightly to the side, he slid out from under me and then lifted me into his arms and onto the bed. After I was situated on my back, he leaned over me. I could see my wetness coating his face as his eyes blazed down at me. He moved slowly, giving me a chance to turn my head before he kissed me, letting me taste myself on his lips. My tongue darted out and he lost control.

"Sexiest fucking thing ever," he growled before he speared inside me with one hard thrust. "But I need to finish inside your pussy this time. Not your mouth."

And with that, he began moving hard and fast, drilling me with each powerful thrust. Over and over again. His strokes ignited little aftershocks in my body, making me scream his name until my voice was hoarse. Finally, when I didn't think I could take any more, he drove deep inside and groaned. The heat from the jets

3

of his semen sparked a fire through every nerve of my body as I panted his name.

"I'm so fucking lucky," he whispered as he swept my dampened hair from my forehead. "I don't know what I ever did to deserve you, but I swear to spend every day for the rest of my life making sure you never regret saying yes."

"I'm lucky too," I rasped out, my chest heaving as I tried to get enough air into my lungs.

"Made for me," he murmured as he pulled me tight.

Resting my head against his chest, I lay there in an exhausted heap and let my thoughts drift again to what people would think about our engagement. I knew we were young and this would shock many of my fellow classmates when we returned to school for our senior year. Surprisingly enough, I didn't think it would surprise my dad too much since he'd been so understanding of my relationship with Drake. More so than I'd ever expected him to be after having seen me with a guy. We'd only met eleven months ago, and this thing between us was about as much of a whirlwind as a romance could be.

When it came down to it, none of that mattered to me. I could hardly wait to become Mrs. Drake Bennett.

CHAPTER 1

Drake

Seventeen long-ass months had passed since I'd slid my ring on Alexa's finger. Five hundred eleven days down and only seven more to go. When I'd proposed to her, I'd known we'd have to wait before I could add the matching wedding band. I'd just figured it would have been over by now. We graduated almost seven months ago, and if I'd had my way, we would have been married shortly after. It had even looked like that was going to happen until my mom had gotten involved and convinced Alexa that it would take months to plan it properly. Once her eyes had lit at the idea of a winter wedding with the possibility of snow and horse-drawn carriages, I hadn't been able to find it in myself to complain too much even though it meant I had to wait for what felt like for-fucking-ever.

Alexa had given up a lot to be with me by agreeing to come back East after graduation so I could try out for one of the best rugby teams in the country. One that everyone thought had the best chance to make it to the Summer Olympics. Her dad had let her bring one of the planes so she could do some charters for him out here, and I'd made sure they had space at the closest airport.

I knew flying was important to her. It was something she and her dad had shared when she was growing up, and it had helped build the bond between them, so I'd tried to make it as easy as possible for her to keep doing it. After a couple of months passed, she started taking the plane up less and less. When I asked her about it, she shrugged it off and said that there weren't enough shorter legs nearby for her to really be of much use to her dad, so he hired another pilot to take the longer overnight trips he couldn't do himself.

I was so busy once I made the team that it was a while before I realized that my mom had practically taken over the planning of the wedding. I tried telling Alexa that it was okay to say no to her, because this was for us and not our parents, but she smiled and said that she enjoyed spending the time with her. It was nice seeing them grow closer, but with my mom in charge the wedding, had turned into a weeklong affair with hundreds of guests. Alexa had explained to me that she liked being able to make my mom happy, and as long as she got to be my wife at the end of it all, it didn't really matter to her if she had to play dress-up for all my parents' friends.

We coasted along for the next couple of months until Alexa started to grow increasingly quiet. I knew something was bothering her. I just couldn't figure out exactly what it was. I had no doubts about her love for me, but there was a distance between us lately, like she was putting up a wall of some kind. One I was determined to tear right back down because I would never tolerate anything coming between the two of us—not even her own stubbornness in holding whatever was bothering her back from me.

Tonight, I was going to get to the bottom of it before Aubrey showed up tomorrow and consumed all of Alexa's time with more wedding stuff. So I grabbed my phone and shot off a text before setting everything up for a romantic dinner for two.

Me: Don't make any dinner plans.

Alexa: Okay. Why?

Me: Because I said so…

Alexa: Who died and made you the boss of me?

Me: Nobody needed to die. I'm already the boss.

Alexa: Really? Says who?

Me: Says you.

Alexa: LOL This oughta be good. How exactly do you figure that?

Me: See that ring on your finger?

Alexa: Yeah… So?

Me: My stamp of ownership.

Alexa: Bahahahaha! NOT!!!

Me: But you're still coming to dinner with me, right?

Alexa: Yes.

Me: Getting my way = I'm the boss.

Alexa: If that's what it takes to make you sleep well at night, who am I to argue?

Me: Love you.

Alexa: Love you too!

My parents let us move into the guesthouse on the property to give us a little more privacy than my room would have allowed. I'd slacked off lately in the romance department, and we hadn't enjoyed a lot of alone time together. Well, other than sex of course. Even with the walls Alexa had erected, she was still mine when we were in bed together each night. It was the only time I felt close to her anymore, and as much of a pussy as it made me sound, it just wasn't enough.

Now, my fucking dreams were full of visions about making her my wife. Me, the guy who used to be able to pick up any chick he wanted at a party to take home for a quick fuck. A tough-as-shit rugby player. All of that ended the moment I laid eyes on Alexa. Now, I just wanted to watch this crazy girl walk down an aisle to me so I could give her my name. And I wanted her to be over-the-fucking-moon happy while she did it. *How sappy is that shit?*

⁓⊱⊶⊰⁓

Glancing at the table, I checked to make sure everything was in order as I heard Alexa's steps nearing the house. Candles were lit. A bottle of her favorite white wine was chilled and ready to go. Our places were set, ready for the food that was staying warm in the oven until it was time to serve it. By the time she got the door open, I had plugged my phone into the sound system so music was playing softly in the background.

"Wow," she murmured as she glanced around the room. "Did I forget a special occasion? It's not your birthday. Or our anniversary."

"I really must be an awful fiancé if I can't surprise you with a nice dinner without having a specific reason for doing so," I told her as I guided her into a chair.

"Not awful. Just a very busy one lately," she corrected me.

I pulled the dishes out of the oven and set them on the table. "That's just it. You should never feel like I'm too busy to make time for you. Especially not right before you're about to marry me. I want us to start off on the right foot with each other, not to act like an old married couple before we've even exchanged our vows."

"I don't think old married couples do what we did to each other last night," she replied before taking a bite of her food,

8

most likely in an attempt to turn the topic of conversation away from anything serious.

Just like I'd allowed her to do for the last month. But not this time.

"I'm serious, Alexa. I need to make sure you know you're the most important thing in my life."

"I do know that," she replied softly, her eyes softening as she set her fork down on her plate.

"Then let's enjoy a nice, quiet meal. Just the two of us," I suggested, wanting her to feel comfortable so she'd open up to me about whatever it was that had been weighing on her mind lately.

Reaching for my fork, I gestured for her to eat too. We chatted about nothing in particular as we took our time with our meal. Once her plate was almost empty, I guided the discussion in the direction it needed to go.

"Everything all set for the wedding next weekend?" I asked. "Anything you'd like my help with?"

The happy smile wiped from her face at my question. Not exactly a good sign. "No," she replied.

"How about for Aubrey's visit? She gets in tomorrow, right?" I pushed, not willing to let the subject drop.

"Yes," she said, giving me a one-word answer again.

"And your dad?"

"He gets in on Wednesday," she offered—five words this time, making it clear that she didn't really want to continue the conversation.

"Do you want to call it all off?" I finally asked the question that had been burning in my brain the last week. "Or do you just have cold feet?"

"Drake!" she gasped. "How can you even ask me that?"

I pulled her hand into mine and held on to it tightly. "Deny it all you want, but something's bothering you. Something you've chosen not to share with me, which makes me think it has to do with me. And as we get closer to the wedding, it's only getting worse. You're here, but you're not exactly with me."

"I'm so sorry I've made you feel like that," she apologized. "I know I'm not the best at opening up, but I've really been trying to do better at it with the big things."

"So this isn't something big?" I asked, not convinced that it could be anything small. Not with the way she'd been acting lately.

After leaving her chair, Alexa climbed onto my lap and pulled my arms around her. "I don't know what I'd call it."

"I need you to try to explain, Alexa," I chided.

"I am. Just give me a second. I'm trying to think of a way that will make sense."

I reached for her face and cupped her cheeks in my palms. "Don't worry about making sense. Talk it through with me instead," I pleaded.

"I keep dreaming of Jackson and Kaylie's wedding day," she began, and I wasn't sure I liked the idea of him starring in her dreams no matter how innocent it was. "It was so peaceful. Just him and Kaylie and the family on a beach in Mexico. Nothing to worry about except celebrating their love."

"It was beautiful," I agreed.

"And I can't shake this feeling that I made a mistake," she continued and my heart dropped.

"A mistake with what?"

"I let our wedding become more about your mom than you

and me," she answered softly. "It's just… She's here when my mom's not. And sharing this with her really has meant the world to me. It's taken away some of the pain I've been feeling about my mom. It's crazy because she died before I ever got the chance to meet her and I've had my whole life to come to terms with her loss, but I miss her more now than I think I ever have before."

"I'm sorry, baby. I know it must be hard for you, thinking about what it would be like if she was here."

"I think I've just been a little sad about it. And that Jackson and Kaylie can't be here with us for the big day because she's too far along in her pregnancy. It's a little weird to think I'm going to be walking down the aisle without the boy who has been like my big brother here," she admitted.

I felt a small twinge of possessiveness at the idea of her missing another guy on our wedding day even though I knew damn well she'd never thought of Jackson as anything other than a friend. And he only had eyes for Kaylie ever since he'd met and fallen for her, realizing what he'd thought he'd felt for Alexa before I'd met her hadn't really been love. But I regretted that circumstances being what they were meant she couldn't have them here for her big day like she wanted. I'd even called Jackson to see if there was anything I could do to get them here, but there was just no way. The timing was too tight since she was so close to the point where she wasn't allowed to fly and the drive was too long for them to do.

"How about we make sure you FaceTime with Jackson and Kaylie the day of the wedding? It won't be exactly the same as them being here, but we can try to do something so they're still part of our day," I suggested.

I loved the way she cocked her head to the side as she thought about my idea. "I like it! I think it might help to be able to see them even if it's through a screen and not in person. I think that, instead of coming to terms with my feelings about my mom and everything, I clung to your mom to make some of the pain go away. But I think I went too far with it, and now, we're having a huge wedding here in your backyard with so many people attending and I feel like it's all spinning out of control."

"And that's it? The reason you've been so distant is the sadness over your mom and the stress of the wedding since my mom turned it into the event of the year?"

"Yes. I swear I didn't even realize I was pushing you away so much. I didn't mean to hurt you. I just let it all get to me and withdrew into my shell a little bit," she explained.

"I know your first instinct when you're hurt or scared is to protect yourself by hiding inside your head, but I need you to let me in there with you too," I said.

"I promise to try, but if you ever feel like I'm shutting you out, please say something right away. It isn't easy breaking a lifetime of habits, so I need your help when you see me slipping at it."

"Sounds like a deal to me," I agreed. "Now, about the wedding… Is there anything you want to change? I know you think it's too late, but it's not. If there's anything you don't like, tell me and I'll fix it."

She smiled brightly up at me, her expression clear of worry for the first time in weeks. "It'll be fine. It's only one week away, so it really is too late to change anything major. Yeah, it will be surrounded by hundreds instead of just our family and friends, but as long as I get to be your wife at the end of the day, then I'm happy."

"Fuck. You have no idea how much I wish you'd told me that

in June."

"Why, so you could whisk me away to Vegas for a quickie wedding?" she teased.

"I would have if I'd known that was even an option," I said, meaning every word of it. "Then I could have spent all these months with my wife under me instead of my fiancée."

The mood between us shifted with my words. Alexa rubbed her thighs together before turning in my lap so she was straddling me.

"How about you show me what you can do with me under you right now?"

"I have a better idea. Why doesn't my fiancée show me what she can do on top of me instead?" I dared her. "Last chance for us to have chair sex out in the open before everyone starts descending upon us until we leave for our honeymoon."

"Chair sex, huh?" she asked in a throaty tone of voice. "I think I could get behind that plan."

I watched as she rose up on her knees so she could wiggle her hips and move her skirt out of the way. She fumbled with my belt and zipper, freeing my cock from the confines of my pants with a determined glint in her eye. Before I realized her intention, she gripped my cock with one hand and sank down on top of me until I was deep inside.

"I want your shirt off too," I growled. "Need to taste your nipples."

"No," she denied me. "I didn't lock the door when I got home and someone could come over at any minute. There isn't a chance in hell I'm pulling off your cock until you make me come, so don't even think about stopping now."

"Alexa," I groaned at the desperation in her voice.

"You wanted to fix something for me. Fix this! I need to come so bad, Drake. Please," she begged.

Hearing her pleading with me for her release pushed me close to the edge of my restraint. I could feel it start to shred as she moved on top of me, slamming herself up and down frantically, already out of control. She was so wet that I could feel the dampness on my pants. The smell of her arousal hit my nose as she grabbed my hair to pull my head closer to hers for a kiss.

Our mouths mimicked the fucking we were doing, our tongues fighting for dominance as I gripped her hips in my fists and tried to control her movements. On each downward stroke, she ground against me until I felt my cock tip nudge against her cervix. I knew she was going to feel it in the morning, but she was so far gone that she didn't seem to care about the bite of pain she must have been feeling.

"Come for me," I urged as I felt her walls tighten around me like a vise.

"Not without you," she whimpered and did that thing where she contracts around me, pumping my shaft in pulses.

"Fuck." I felt a tingle in my spine that radiated to my balls. "Wanted to make it last."

"And I want it hard and fast," she countered.

I took her at her word and hammered up into her body over and over again. Our hips slammed against each other, and I could hear the slapping of our skin as we made contact.

"You first," I insisted right before I moved my hand so I could reach her clit and rubbed it in circular motions.

Her pussy clamped down immediately and fluttered around me as she came. She collapsed against my body as I surged upward one last time and planted myself deep inside as I let go too. Jets of semen spurted from my cock, leaving us with a mess when I finally lifted her off me and onto her unsteady feet.

I grabbed a napkin from the table and cleaned us both off before picking her limp body up and carrying her to our room. I hadn't cooked the meal, so there wasn't much to clean up. It could wait until morning. Getting my girl to bed couldn't.

CHAPTER 2

Alexa

After I slept well for the first night in ages, morning rolled around quickly, and it was almost time for Aubrey to arrive. When I heard the car pull up in the driveway, I threw the door open and ran outside. As soon as she stepped out of the car, I gathered Aubrey to me for a hug and never wanted to let go.

"I'm so glad you're finally here!"

"Me too. I've missed you so much. We've never spent so much time away from each other," she whispered in my ear. "Not since we met back in kindergarten."

"But now you have a life to build with Luka in Chicago and I have one here with Drake," I sighed before stepping away.

"We just need to take advantage of that pilot's license of yours once you get past the wedding so you can come visit more often," she said. "FaceTime and Facebook just don't cut it all the time. Sometimes, I miss your real face and need that instead. And not just for things like bachelorette parties!"

The last time I'd seen Aubrey was when we'd both flown back to our hometown so she could throw my bachelorette party. Old friends from high school and college joined us for a fun night on the town, including our roommates Faith and Natalie from junior year. I spent the night drinking, dancing, and listening to them complain about how there were no good men left after Aubrey and I had snapped up Drake and Luka.

We spent most of the time at The Rooster's Nest, and Kaylie made sure we got the best service possible since she used to bartend there. She kept ordering me shots with crazy names, which was terribly unfair because I couldn't get my revenge since she was pregnant. By the time the night was over, we were all trashed and Kaylie had to call Jackson to help get everybody home even though we'd hired a limousine. It was probably the best part of the whole wedding process so far because I didn't have to lift a finger except to knock back some drinks. Although I did draw the line at wearing that 'suck for a buck' shirt Aubrey had brought with her.

I tipped the driver and thanked him as he removed her luggage from the trunk before getting back in the limo and driving away. When I turned back to Aubrey, I saw the telltale twinkle on her ring finger as she reached down for one of her bags.

"Ohimgod!" I shrieked, snatching her hand up so I could see the ring. "You're engaged! You didn't tell me Luka proposed. Why didn't you tell me?"

"Because you haven't given me a chance to yet," she giggled. "I've barely said hello."

"So what happened? How did he ask?" I demanded. "You have to tell me everything!"

"Help me haul all this to my room and I'll tell you anything you want to know," she promised.

I grabbed two bags, practically ran for the door, and raced up the stairs. Aubrey wasn't far behind me, and I slammed the door shut as soon as she entered the room.

"Okay, spill."

She threw herself onto the bed and heaved a deep sigh. "It was so romantic. Almost like something out of a movie," she began with a dreamy look on her face, her eyes staring up at the ceiling and a goofy grin spread across her lips. "Luka was so upset that he couldn't come early with me, but since he just got that promotion last month, it was impossible for him to take the whole week off."

"Yeah, yeah. C'mon. Get to the good stuff," I urged.

"Well, he insisted upon taking me to the airport this morning. O'Hare is always a mess, so he dropped me off at the door and had a skycap check in my luggage. I was halfway through the security line when my cell phone started to ring with a call from him. I thought he was just checking to make sure everything was going smoothly, but he told me I'd forgotten something important and he'd bring it inside."

"You never forget anything. You're too organized for that," I pointed out.

"I tried to ask him what it was, but the call disconnected, so I stepped out of line. I was dreading the idea of starting all over again when Luka came rushing up," she said.

"And then?" I asked.

"He took my hands in his, dropped to one knee, and told me I'd forgotten to promise to be his forever and asked if I would marry him. That he couldn't let me get on the plane without knowing I wanted to spend the rest of my life with him."

"Wow," I sighed.

"Yeah. I was so surprised that I didn't even remember to answer until people surrounding us started yelling encouragement," she giggled.

I could practically picture it in my mind, and she'd been right when she'd said that it was like a scene from one of those sappy movies she liked to watch all the time.

"So it's safe to assume you said yes?"

"Of course I did," she huffed. "And I bawled my eyes out when he told me he'd bought the ring months ago and was just waiting for the right time to ask. Then he apologized for messing up and not giving me the romantic proposal of my dreams."

"Are you ever going to clue him in and let him know he nailed the proposal perfectly?" I asked.

"Sure," she answered. "Sometime in the next fifty years or so."

We giggled like we used to when we were little girls and stared down at the rings on each of our fingers.

"We get to trade places next time. You'll be the bride and I'll be the maid of honor."

"I don't know. Maybe Luka and I will just skip the big wedding thing and elope in Vegas or something."

I laughed at the idea of Aubrey agreeing to elope. "After all the times you talked me into playing wedding, there's no way I can see that happening."

"Well, let's see how hard this wedding stuff is when we aren't playing make-believe and I'll let you know later," she said. "From the sound of our last call, I expect there's a list a mile long of things we still need to do."

Truer words had never been said. After Aubrey unpacked and we had a quick bite to eat, we tackled the big items on my to-do list. After six hours, our mad dash of errands was finally coming to a close. We'd already stopped at the florist, the bakery, and the salon. My hair was swept into an up-do I loved and my makeup was done. And now, it was the moment of truth—time to try on my wedding dress. Drake's mom, Grace, met us at the store so she could try on her dress as well since it needed to be hemmed.

19

I stepped into the gown, and the seamstress, Jennifer, helped me with the laces in the back. The alterations seemed to have worked because the fit in the bodice was now perfect. Locking my eyes with Aubrey after leaving the dressing room and moving to the mirrors, I noticed the stunned expression on her face as she saw me in my wedding gown for the first time. She hadn't been able to make it out when I'd gone shopping for it, so Drea had come with me instead. Grace was nowhere in sight right now, so this moment was just for the two of us.

The dress was unlike anything I ever expected to wear in my life. When Drea had talked me into trying it on, I'd only agreed so she'd leave me alone. But the moment I saw myself in this dress I fell in love with it. It was ivory silk organza with a natural waist and an embroidered lace overlay over the bodice that flowed into long sleeves. The combination of skin and lace on the illusion neckline made me feel beautiful and sexy. Then when the sales lady explained the dress had been inspired by Grace Kelly's wedding gown, I knew I had to have it.

"Lexi!" Aubrey exclaimed. "You look so beautiful. The pictures you sent were great, but they still didn't do the dress justice. It's like it was made for you."

"It really is perfect, isn't it?" I sighed as I turned this way and that to see myself from different angles.

"Yes, it is," she agreed. "For a girl I usually have to force into a dress practically kicking and screaming, you sure went all out on this one."

"Because she had to," someone said nastily. "Although you can dress up a pig as much as you'd like, but everyone still knows it's a pig—lipstick and all."

I locked eyes with Sasha in the mirror before turning to face her. Seeing Aubrey take a step forward in anger, I grabbed her arm to hold her back. Then I shook my head when she turned and gave me an exasperated look. Stepping in front of Aubrey, I confronted Sasha myself. This was a battle I needed to fight on my own.

"Go away," I growled. "You aren't going to ruin anything else for me ever again, so you might as well just leave now before you make a fool of yourself."

She flipped her long, blond hair over her shoulder before replying. "Oh, please. I'm not the one who's making a fool of herself. You are if you think people are going to accept you around here just because you're marrying into the Bennett family. They can dress you up so you look the part, but you'll never be accepted as one of us."

"You can take your acceptance and shove it," I retorted. "I don't need it. I'll take Drake as my husband instead and you can just keep on being a bitter, spoiled little rich girl."

"He may be marrying you this weekend, but don't think for a minute that means he's going to be yours forever. It doesn't take much for men like him and Jackson to stray."

"Whatever," I scoffed. "I have no worries about Drake straying, and Jackson isn't going anywhere. Not with his ring on Kaylie's finger and his baby in her belly."

Sasha paled at my words before her eyes narrowed and her chin lifted. I might have felt bad for her and her unrequited feelings for Jackson if she weren't such a bitch.

"Fine," she huffed. "Maybe Kaylie will be able to hold on to Jackson because she managed to get knocked up, but that doesn't mean you'll hold Drake's interest forever. Unless this is a shotgun wedding too?"

"You know this ring has been on my finger for a year and half, Sasha," I reminder her, waving my fingers in her face. "The only way this could be a shotgun wedding was if I were a freaking elephant."

"Get your fingers out of my face!" she shrieked, pushing my hand away.

"Oh hell no," I heard Aubrey say as she tried to push past me.

Reaching my arms out, I pushed both girls back and away from each other.

"You can't push me," Sasha hissed, grabbing the sleeve of my dress and pulling.

The second I heard the sound of tearing fabric, a red haze settled over my vision.

"You bitch!" I snarled before throwing a right hook that connected with her face. I watched her drop, blood spurting from her nose, and was about to step forward when Grace intervened.

"Enough," she said sternly. "Alexa, go change out of your gown so they can see how much damage has been done."

"But—" I sputtered before she interrupted me.

"Go. We don't want you to get any blood on you, because I have no idea how they'd get the stain out of that material," she said, shooing me away with her hands.

Aubrey stepped to my side and pulled me towards the dressing room, but I stopped because I wanted to know what Grace was going to say to Sasha. My fear was that she was angry with me over this confrontation and it would damage our relationship. Luckily, it was a fear that she quickly put to rest.

"Let's get you up," she sighed before reaching down to help Sasha onto her feet as Jennifer brought some tissues over.

"She broke my nose!" Sasha cried. "I'm gonna call the police!"

"No, you're not," Drake's countered. "Because then Jennifer,

Aubrey, and I will all have to tell them that you started the fight."

"But that would be a lie," she argued. "I didn't start the fight. I never even hit her."

"Your mother will be so disappointed in you when she hears about this stunt. You chose to interrupt what should have been a happy day for Alexa and turned it into something horrible. You smacked her hand away and pulled on her dress. You damaged it for God's sake. I saw you. I heard every single word you said. What the hell were you thinking?"

I was as stunned as Sasha appeared to be to learn that she'd listened to our entire exchange.

"I... You... We..." she stammered.

"The whole thing, Sasha," she stressed. "At first, I thought I must have been imagining things because there's no way the girl I know would have done something like this. By the time I realized you truly were attacking my daughter-in-law in a bridal shop while she was trying on her dress, you were on the ground bleeding. Needless to say, your behavior means there's no way you or your family will be at any of the wedding events this week."

"But my mom will be so upset!" Sasha wailed, finally realizing the ramifications of what she'd done.

"Yes, because of you, my best friend will not be there when my only son gets married. I'm terribly disappointed, but I won't for a minute do anything to make Alexa feel uncomfortable on her wedding day. Just as you should have never tried to hurt her feelings today. Unfortunately, your mother and I will both have to pay for your mistaken judgment," she said, shaking her head sadly.

"I'm sorry," she apologized. "I never meant for it to go so far."

23

"You never did mean for things to go as far as they did when you were younger either. Eventually, you are going to have to grow up, and I can only hope that, this time around, your parents properly punish you for the damage you've caused here today," she replied.

"You can't really mean that. You're my godmother. You've always stood up for me, and now, you're just taking her side," Sasha complained.

"I'm not choosing sides, Sasha. You still have so much growing up to do if you really think that's what this is," Grace explained. "What you did here today was spiteful. And just flat-out wrong. Drake adores Alexa, and so does the rest of our family. She's already been accepted by everyone who counts. She doesn't need to prove anything to anyone else."

Sasha's shoulders dropped in defeat. "I really am sorry."

"And if you really meant that, you'd be asking for Alexa's forgiveness instead of mine. That's the second time you've said the words, and both times, they've been directed to the wrong person. Now go before I do something rash like call the police myself," she said, ordering Sasha out of the shop with a finger pointed at the door.

After Sasha's departure, Grace turned back to me.

"I have no doubt Drake will do everything in his power to ensure he remains at your side for the rest of his life just like his father has done with me. Don't ever doubt his love for you."

"I won't," I swore.

"Good. Now let's see how much damage was done to your gorgeous dress. Jennifer, can the sleeve be repaired?" she asked the seamstress.

Jennifer examined the gown and muttered under her breath, "With the way it tore, I just can't be certain. She'll have to leave it here and I'll see what can be done, but our safest bet this close to the wedding may be to alter it into cap sleeves or something. I'm just not sure I have enough extra fabric from the alterations to make a whole new sleeve if that's what it comes down to."

I looked to Aubrey for help since most of what Jennifer had said had flown right over my head. I was trying desperately not to cry at the thought of my gown being ruined.

"Go ahead," she urged me. "Get changed back into your clothes, and I promise you we'll fix this so you are even more stunning on your wedding day than when you walked out of the changing room here. Trust me."

"Trust both of us," Grace offered. "We have this under control."

What other choice do I have but to agree?

As I stripped out of the dress in which I'd felt like the most beautiful woman minutes ago, a tear slid down my cheek. Sometimes, I didn't even recognize myself anymore. I'd agreed to a wedding that required me to dress up night after night while we entertained guests, and I normally hated getting all fancied up. It was weighing on my mind enough that I now had recurring dreams about Jackson's simple beach wedding because my envy over it was eating me alive.

Even worse, I missed my mom so damn much that sometimes I felt like my heart was breaking, but I hadn't said a word to my fiancé about it until he'd forced me to do so—even though I'd promised him during our one and only huge blowout fight that I wouldn't keep secrets from him. And now, in a dress shop, I'd gotten into a fight that had damaged the ridiculously expensive gown I was supposed to wear as I walked down the aisle.

When I'd told Drake that I felt like things were spinning out of control, I'd had no idea it would ever get this bad. I'd never hit another person in my life, and I wasn't happy that I'd felt the need to do so now when I was the damn center of attention already because I was the bride-to-be. I certainly wasn't acting like the blushing bride lately.

CHAPTER 3

Drake

"What the fuck happened?" I growled into the phone, stunned at what my mom was telling me. I wanted to drive over to Sasha's house and ream her a new one for having hurt Alexa, but I knew it wouldn't solve anything. Her spoiled ass would probably have appreciated the attention even if it was negative.

"Don't use that language with me," my mom snipped back. "I had no idea Sasha was going to pull a stunt like this, but I've taken care of it."

I took a few deep breaths, trying to calm myself down. I couldn't picture Alexa punching anybody—let alone one of my childhood friends in a dress shop with my mom less than a week before the wedding. I'd cut off all contact with Sasha after the shit she pulled with us our junior year. We might have grown up playing together since our moms were best friends, but I wasn't quick to forgive or forget the fact that her meddling had almost cost me my relationship with Alexa. There was no way in hell I was going to let her fuck with my woman again—not after last time when I flew off the handle and allowed her little rumor-building efforts to cause a huge fight between Alexa and me.

"Mom, thank you for being there when Alexa needed you," I finally said once I was less agitated. "But you need to know I won't put up with this bullshit. Not even for a minute. I know this might be hard for you to hear, but Sasha isn't welcome in my life anymore. At all. Not even for you or out of respect for your friendship with her mom."

"Drake," she sighed. "When it comes down to it, Alexa is family. She's going to be your wife. Eventually, she will be the mother of my grandchildren. Family comes first. Always."

"Then you know what I have to do," I told her.

"I've already done it," she assured me. "Sasha has been told neither she nor her parents are welcome at the wedding festivities. My next call after talking to you is going to be to her mom to let her know what happened. I would have called her first, but the last thing I wanted was for somebody to hear what happened and get to you before I did, because then I knew you'd go off half-cocked and do something stupid."

"You can't make that promise, Mom. You don't understand. She's in a vulnerable place right now and it's my job to protect her. A job I haven't done very well lately," I admitted.

"You had no way of knowing something like this was going to happen today. And she's not as fragile as you think, son. She managed to break Sasha's nose with one punch," my mom pointed out.

I couldn't help but feel a little proud that she'd popped Sasha one like that. "Did she hurt her hand? Did you take her to the doctor to have an x-ray done just in case?"

"Her hand is fine, Drake. She didn't hurt herself and she doesn't need to get it checked out," my mom assured me.

"Are you sure? Because she's the type to suffer in silence if she's embarrassed by what happened. It might be hurting and you don't know."

"That's it. I'm putting Alexa on the phone. Maybe she can talk some sense into you," she said before I heard some muttering in the background and Alexa's voice came on the line.

"Drake, I really am fine," she insisted. "I'm sorry I made such a scene at the shop, but you don't need to worry about my hand. Those self-defense lessons Jackson insisted Aubrey and I take years ago were finally put to good use. I remembered exactly how to make a fist so I wouldn't get hurt."

"Baby, I'm sorry I wasn't there to protect you. Sasha never should have been there," I apologized.

"It's a dress shop. Women go there to buy stuff, and we both know how much she likes to spend money," Alexa reasoned with me. "I'm sure it wasn't planned and was a total coincidence."

"Still, I don't like it," I grumbled.

Alexa's voice dropped to a whisper. "Neither do I, but it is what it is. She pushed my buttons, I broke her nose, and your mom disinvited her and her parents from our wedding. If anything, I feel bad for your mom because I could tell it killed her to have to do that."

"Baby, how many times do I have to tell you? This wedding is about you and me. Nobody else," I growled into the phone. "Say it back to me. Now!"

"This wedding is about you and me and nobody else," she repeated.

"If anyone does anything at any time this week that you don't like, I want you to remind yourself of those words. It's our new mantra. Got it?"

Her giggles filtered through the line and the tension in my body started to seep away.

"We have a mantra now?"

"Yes. For this one week plus our honeymoon, the world revolves around us. And after that, my world will still revolve around you," I reminded her. "Always and forever."

"Love you," she whispered back.

"Good. Then get your butt home. Your dad got into town and he's staring at me with laser-beam eyes because I think he heard me say you punched someone. I may need you to come rescue me before he beats me up for letting his baby girl get into a fistfight," I teased.

"Drake!" she gasped in a horrified tone.

"Too early for jokes?" I asked. Her silence was enough of an answer for me. "Okay, just hurry back because I miss you."

"We're on our way already," she replied before disconnecting the call.

"Sounds like my little girl got into some trouble in town," her dad said from behind me.

I'd asked him to meet me in the guesthouse so we could talk as soon as he got settled in. I'd been hoping he'd be able to help me find a way for Alexa to feel connected to her mom this week, but we'd been interrupted by my mom's call as soon as he'd arrived.

"Yeah, you could say that again," I agreed before explaining what had happened with Sasha.

"Ex-girlfriend?" he wanted to know when I was done. He looked pissed at the idea of Alexa paying for one of my past mistakes.

"No, we never dated. You have Jackson to thank for the amount of anger Sasha still holds against Alexa, although they technically didn't date either. That and the fact her parents spoiled the hell out of her growing up."

"Consider this a lesson learned then," he told me. "I know you can provide well for my daughter and any children the two of you have, but don't forget the important things in life. You make sure they know that the real things in life can't be bought and family comes first."

"I will," I swore. "My parents taught Drea and me that lesson well while we were growing up."

"I know they raised you well. If they hadn't, I wouldn't have let you get close to my daughter. I'm glad I trusted my intuition and didn't interfere in your courtship," he admitted.

"You went beyond not interfering," I said. "There were times you flat-out helped my cause. And I need your help now."

"I'm assuming it's about Alexa since you wanted to speak with me before she got back" he asked. "If there's something she needs, you know you don't ever have to ask for my help. Just tell me what you need me to do."

I went on to explain the conversation I'd had with Alexa the previous night and the things that were weighing on her mind—her mother in particular. "This week should be one of Alexa's happiest times, but she's been so damn sad. Is there anything you can think of to help her feel that connection? I don't know how to help her get past this."

Her dad was looking down at the ground, his head resting in his hands as he listened to me. When he lifted his head to look at me, there were tears in his eyes.

"I brought something that might help," he offered. "I'd planned to give them to her on her wedding day so she'd have something of her mom's with her as she walked down the aisle. A piece of jewelry I've been holding on to for this very occasion. But if you think she needs it sooner, then of course I'll give it to her now."

I thought about it for a moment and came to a decision, one I hoped I wouldn't regret later. "Not yet. She finally opened up to me last night. I think it helped a little, sharing the burden with me. And now you, Aubrey and her parents are all here to offer support. That might just be enough for her to focus on the positive until the wedding day."

"And I hope she doesn't get into any more fistfights," he joked in an attempt to lighten the mood.

"I wouldn't bring that up with her if I were you. She didn't seemed too pleased when I tried to make a joke out of it. Too soon yet," I warned.

"Well, then let me rephrase that. Let's hope nothing else goes wrong and all the bad luck is out of the way for the week," he corrected his earlier statement.

Too bad it wasn't an accurate prediction of what would happen in the days that followed.

CHAPTER 4

Alexa

Everything seemed to settle down for the next few days. Guests started trickling in from out of town, and I got to meet more of Drake's extended family. It was a little weird for me since mine was so small. I wasn't accustomed to family get-togethers that included almost a hundred people, but his family was huge when you included all the aunts, uncles, nieces, nephews, and cousins, and that's how many of them would be here by the time our wedding day arrived. It was going to take some getting used to, but it was also a comfort to know that they were all so welcoming.

All the details for the wedding finally seemed to be coming together smoothly for a change too. Or maybe it was just me who had changed now that I was reminded daily of our new 'world revolving around us' mantra by Drake. Although he kept an eagle eye on me too, so it's not like I had a choice but to chill out about the preparations. After the fight with Sasha, he barely let me out of his sight. With him by my side, I felt like nothing could possibly go wrong and started to relax so I could enjoy the festivities too.

Having Aubrey and her mom here really made a difference. Both of them stepped in and handled any of the million little things that could have gone wrong, shielding me from all the stress. Aubrey insisted it was all part of her maid of honor duties. She knew me so well that she didn't even have to come to me with most of the questions either. There was a definite advantage to having a best friend who'd known me practically forever. And since she'd bought into Drake's mantra too, she wasn't letting anything that could have possibly irritated me reach my ears.

Before I knew it, we only had two more days to go. Forty-eight hours until I walked down the aisle and became Mrs. Drake Bennett. I was so excited that I could hardly wait. Tomorrow was the rehearsal and dinner, so Aubrey was raiding my closet to make sure she approved of the outfit I'd chosen to wear.

"You really did go all out on the clothes shopping," I heard her mumble as she rifled through the hangers.

"Not me. Grace and Drea," I explained.

"Ahhh, that makes much more sense. I was beginning to wonder if you'd gotten a personality transplant and you were already spending your hubby's money like a wild woman," she teased. "Well, you are going to look amazing this weekend, and you have plenty of things to wear for the honeymoon, too."

"Yeah, if only I knew what to pack for it," I complained.

Aubrey's head peeked out of the closet as she swiveled to look at me. "Drake still hasn't spilled the beans on where you're going?"

"No. He was only willing to tell me to pack lots of lingerie and bikinis," I said, shaking my head in frustration. I was so not good with surprises, and it was driving me crazy that he insisted on keeping this a secret from me.

"He's being pretty brave springing a surprise honeymoon on you," she said, laughing a little because she knew better than almost anyone else how hard it was for me.

I heard a buzzing sound and pulled her cell from her purse since she'd thrown it on the bed and made no move to leave the closet. She was too busy sorting through all my new purchases. If I left her to it, she'd end up packing for the honeymoon too, and I didn't want to disturb her too much since that would be awesome. When I glanced down, I noticed that it was a text from Jackson.

"Hey, it looks like your brother is trying to get ahold of you," I told her as I tossed the phone her way.

"Oh, no," Aubrey whispered as she checked her text message.

"What's wrong?" I asked, worried by how freaked out she appeared.

Aubrey looked up at me and there were tears in her eyes. "They had to put Kaylie on bed rest."

My heart dropped at the news that something was wrong with the pregnancy. "How bad is it? Did he give you any details?"

"He just got off the phone with Mom and Dad, and it says they have all the details. All he told me is she's already three centimeters dilated and ninety percent effaced. I don't even know what that means except she needs to stay off her feet until she gives birth," she explained.

"But isn't it too early? She still has almost a month to go before her due date," I asked.

"I know," Aubrey sighed. "But it sounds like my niece got her patience from her daddy and doesn't want to wait."

Problems with pregnancies scared the living daylights out of me. I knew things had changed a lot medically since I was born twenty-two years ago, but this wasn't something I could think about rationally. My heart ruled over my head on this topic as thoughts of my mom's death haunted me.

"Let's go find your parents then and see if they have more information," I urged.

Aubrey's hand trembled as she held mine while we walked down the hall to their guest room. Their door was cracked open slightly, and we could hear them talking as we neared it.

"I don't know what to do!" Aubrey's mom cried out, sounding devastated. "I know Lexi needs me here. She's like a second daughter to me and I love her as much as my own children. How could I not? She stole a piece of my heart the morning Aubrey and I met her."

"I know you love her, honey," Aubrey's dad reassured her. "We all do."

"But Jackson needs me too," she continued.

"He told you himself that you should stay until after the wedding. The doctors told him bed rest should work and you know he isn't going to let her out of that bed for anything," he reminded her.

Trying to give them some more time to discuss this without us interfering, I tugged at Aubrey's hand to stop her. Instead of stopping, she shook her head no and dragged me closer.

"They won't want to tell us anything if it's bad," she whispered.

"Jackson doesn't want to ruin Lexi's day," Aubrey's mom retorted. "And that's exactly what would happen if I leave now. But how will I ever forgive myself if Kaylie goes into premature labor and something goes wrong?"

"You heard what he said. The doctors are worried there's a small risk she might go into labor and want to do everything they can to get her to thirty-six weeks first. But there's no way to know for sure if she's going to go into labor early," he said, attempting to soothe her.

"She's dilated, effaced, and lost her mucus plug already!" she shrieked. "Those are all signs of labor."

"Calm down. Getting upset like this isn't going to help anything. You were dilated with each of the boys for weeks before you gave birth. It was only with Aubrey that everything went so quickly," he reminded her. "And if the worst-case scenario happens, we can get you on a plane and home in a few hours easily."

"Not easily," she argued. "I can't exactly ask the bride or her father to pilot a plane in the middle of the wedding festivities."

"Shit," he sighed. "I'll talk to Nick and see if he can get one of his pilots out here just in case we need one. It's ironic that he and Lexi are both pilots with planes at their disposal and they are the last people we can ask right now."

Aubrey's skin paled as she clenched my hand while we listened to her parents' conversation.

"Go in and talk to them," I urged her quietly.

"Come with me," she asked as she tugged me with her.

I pulled my hand away and shook my head. "No, your parents need you. Go on," I insisted until she turned away from me and lightly knocked on the door.

As soon as she walked into the room, I raced away and ran straight to the guesthouse. Right past Drake and up the stairs into our room. I dove for the bed and buried my head in a pillow as the tears I'd managed to hold inside poured from my eyes. Sobs racked my body and I couldn't stop shaking.

Drake wasn't far behind me. I heard his swift footsteps as he followed me into the room and his swearing as I crumbled.

"Fuck, baby," he breathed out as he climbed into bed next to me. "What happened?"

"Kaylie's on bed rest," I whimpered.

"Are she and the baby okay?"

"I don't know for sure. It sounded like maybe just a precaution, but what if it's not? What if she goes into labor while everyone is here and something goes wrong?" I asked as I began to panic.

"Then we'll figure something out," he promised me. "But let's not borrow trouble, baby. You need to calm down. You aren't going to do anyone any good if you make yourself sick. Shhh, baby. Everything will be okay."

"You don't know that, Drake. Nobody knows. When my mom went into labor with me, I'm sure my dad thought everything as going to be okay and she died," I whispered. "People die when they have babies. It happens. Even now, twenty-two years later."

"Yes, sometimes it does. And sometimes planes crash, but you love to fly," he pointed out. "Life's about risk, and I'm sure Kaylie and Jackson are doing everything they can to limit the chances of anything bad happening and are focused on the fact that the baby will be here soon."

"What if I'm never brave enough to try?" I softly admitted. It was one of my biggest fears, something we'd never talked about before now but should have if we were going to be married.

"Try what?" he asked, not understanding what I meant.

"What if I'm too scared to get pregnant and decide that I never want to have children? Would you still be happy with me?" I worried aloud.

"Alexa," he sighed as he gathered me close. Tears were still streaming down my cheeks. "Yes. No matter what, I want you to be my wife. It seems like I've waited forever to be able to introduce you to people as my wife, and it's not something I will ever regret. If we have children, don't have children, or even adopt some, as long as I have you, I'll have exactly what I want."

"God, I'm sorry I'm such a mess lately. It just feels like it's all going to hell," I cried, a little hiccup in my voice as I tried to catch my breath again. "My dress had to be changed because Sasha ruined one of the sleeves and I have no idea how it's really going to look. And now, a million people will be here but not all the people who are most important to me because I need to make sure Aubrey and her parents get on a plane in the morning. Kaylie and the baby are more important. They need to be there to make sure nothing bad happens. Jackson needs his family."

"Close your eyes, baby. You're exhausted. Everything will seem better in the morning," he whispered as he rubbed my back with light circles.

"I don't see how, Drake," I sighed as the adrenaline left my system and my eyes started drifting closed.

"You leave that to me," I heard as his lips caressed my forehead in a light kiss before he pulled me closer.

With his warmth and strength surrounding me, I fell asleep thinking there was no way to solve this problem. I was going to be married in two days with nobody but my father to represent my family.

CHAPTER 5

Drake

Seeing the tears that streaked Alexa's face even while she slept broke my heart. All I'd ever wanted was her happiness. Nothing else really mattered, and I felt like I'd watched her struggle long enough. Now was time for action. Rolling out of bed, I moved as quietly and quickly as I could. I had a lot to do before morning if I was going to pull this off.

I threw on some clothes and grabbed my phone to fire off a few texts while I was on my way to the main house. By the time I got there, everyone was gathered in the kitchen. All eyes turned to me, and I could tell they were confused by my request to meet.

"Alexa shared with me the news about the Kaylie's bed rest and how she feels like you need to go back now in case anything goes wrong," I told Aubrey and her parents.

Mr. and Mrs. Silver looked at each other before he spoke. "We talked to Jackson and Kaylie tonight and decided we should stay until after the wedding. It's only a couple more days, and Kaylie isn't having any contractions yet."

"While I appreciate your willingness to stay for Alexa, she would never forgive herself if something went wrong," I explained. "I don't think you realize how tightly wound she's been the last few months, and this struck her deep."

"Because of the way we lost her mom," her dad interjected softly, his eyes meeting mine in understanding.

"Yes," I confirmed. "The wedding already made her miss her mom even more than normal, and then to have an issue with Kaylie's pregnancy? It has her terrified."

"Megan and I can talk to her in the morning and alleviate some of her worries," my mom said as she looked at Mrs. Silver, who nodded her head in agreement.

"Bed rest isn't a bad thing. The doctors just want to be careful so the baby can get closer to full term. In a couple of weeks, they'll take her off the restriction once it's safer for the baby to be born," Mrs. Silver explained.

"I don't think she's thinking clearly," I replied, shaking my head. "She already heard you and your husband talking and has it set in her mind that there's a problem and she needs to fix it."

"She did?" she asked.

"Yes, Mom," Aubrey confirmed. "She didn't want to come in because she said we needed to talk as a family, but we both heard your conversation before I knocked. It was pretty scary stuff, even for me, and I don't have the same issues with childbirth that Lexi does because of her mom's death."

"Which means she didn't have a chance to hear what your mom had to say after she calmed down, thought it through more clearly, and stopped panicking," Aubrey's dad realized out loud.

"And by the time she made it to the guesthouse, she was practically inconsolable. That's why I think this calls for drastic measures," I said, leading into my crazy idea.

My dad nodded his head in encouragement, and I knew that, no matter what I said next, I at least had his support already.

"By the time Alexa wakes up, I want everything ready so I can fly her back home."

"So she can see Kaylie and Jackson for herself? Can I come too?" Aubrey asked excitedly.

"We don't have time for you guys to take a trip tomorrow, Drake," my mom argued. "You have the rehearsal starting at four, dinner right after, and then the ceremony is the next day."

41

"And that's why I'm going to need all of your help to pull this off," I said.

"I'll do whatever you need if you think it will help my baby girl," Alexa's dad offered.

"Pull what off?" Aubrey's mom asked, looking around the room in confusion.

"I'm going to change a few things for our wedding day," I began.

"Unless this trip is extremely quick or your plan involves skipping the rehearsal entirely, I just don't see how this will work. And how will we make the changes if you two aren't even here to run things by?" my mom asked.

"Ohmigod!" Aubrey gasped as she must have realized where I was going with this.

Both men in the room were grinning at everyone's reactions, and I thought they must have figured out part of my plan too. I took it as a good sign that neither of them were yelling yet since they were paying for the events we already had planned here.

"The things I'm changing are pretty major and require both of us to be back in Alexa's hometown," I replied. "Because that's where we're going to exchange our vows."

My mom leapt from her chair and started pacing the room. "We have hundreds of guests coming for your wedding, Drake! You can't just change the location to someplace several states away days before the one day before!"

"When the girl I'm going to marry is a licensed pilot and so is her dad, I can," I argued reasonably. "And I am going to do it because this is what's best for Alexa."

"Calm down, honey. Let our boy explain what he wants before you fly off the handle," my dad interjected.

"I want Alexa to be able to marry me in a place where she's surrounded by her loved ones," I said as I looked towards Aubrey and her parents. "Without feeling guilty about them being there."

"Before you make a rash decision, let me talk to her when she wakes up and reassure her that there's no need to feel guilty," Mrs. Silver said.

Shaking my head, I looked at Alexa's dad next. "And I want her to feel closer to her mom too. As morbid as it sounds to start our wedding day in a cemetery, I want her to be able to put flowers on her mom's grave before she walks down the aisle to me. So her mom is a part of our special day even though she's gone. And the only way that can happen is if we go back."

Alexa's dad's eyes were filled with sadness as he returned my stare. "My gift will help her feel closer to her mom," he reminded me.

"I know, but I think she needs more. Plus, if we do this at the Silvers' house, then Jackson could be there too. And she's been sad that he won't be here for her wedding day too," I said, explaining the last reason why I thought this was the right decision.

"How can we possibly move everything though?" my mom asked.

"That's the beauty of my plan. We don't have to move everything—just the rehearsal and the ceremony. We can fly in tomorrow and take care of any details we can't do over the phone. Then we get married in the morning and fly back for the reception," I told them.

"I have room for all of us on the plane," Alexa's dad said.

"And the flight's only a couple of hours. If we time it right, the reception can happen without any changes at all, Mom," I pleaded with her, hoping she'd agree.

"I think I know someone who can tape the ceremony so your guests can watch it from here if you wanted," Aubrey offered. "I can make some calls and find a place that will set up a projection screen so everyone can see it."

"But we'd be abandoning everyone here," my mom worried. "How will we explain this if we're all gone?"

"I'm sure your sister will be happy to be left in charge while we're gone," my dad told her.

"Yeah. Aunt Marci would be perfect. You know she'll be happy to help," I agreed.

"It doesn't matter what I come up with, does it? You're going to have a solution for everything?" she asked me.

Nodding my head as I walked towards her, I looked down at my mom so she'd see how serious I was. "Yes, and if I don't, I know you'll help me find one. Because this is what's best for Alexa. And I grew up watching you and dad doing anything you needed to do to make each other happy. To make Drea and me happy."

She started crying, and I hugged her close. "Well, I can't exactly argue with that now can I?"

"Nope, you can't," I said.

"Well, then I guess I better get to work so we'll be ready to leave in the morning," she said.

"Can you let Drea know about the change when she gets back?" I asked. "When I texted her, she told me she was visiting a friend in town."

"Sure, honey," she agreed. "I'll make sure your sister is ready for the flight in the morning too. And as long as she's there already, I'll call the owner of the dress shop and ask her to meet Drea there so she can pick up Alexa's dress. They finished the additional alterations this afternoon and we were supposed to go back in the morning to get it."

"Thanks, Mom," I said as I gave her one last squeeze before letting go.

We spent the next thirty minutes running through the list of things that needed to be done in the next twenty-four hours if I hoped to pull this off. Once we divided everything up, they began leaving one by one to get a start on their lists until it was just Alexa's dad and me left.

"Thank you for loving her so much. For moving Heaven and Earth to make sure she has everything she could ever need. You are exactly what her mom would have wished for our baby girl," her dad murmured as he patted me on the back before walking out of the kitchen.

I took a moment to let his approval soak in before I shook it off. I needed to get moving too because I had a ton of stuff to do before Alexa woke up. Then I needed to convince her to agree to this plan too. Hopefully the toughest task on my list wasn't going to be getting her to agree to this plan. Alexa and surprises usually didn't go well together, and this was going to be one hell of a shock.

CHAPTER 6

Alexa

"C'mon, baby," Drake whispered in my ear.

I stretched and rolled over before I remembered everything that had happened in the last week. Wanting nothing more than to block it all out, I pulled the covers over my head.

"No," I grumbled. "I know I'm supposed to be doing a million and one things before the rehearsal, but I just can't do it. I think I'm just going to spend the day in bed instead. It's not like things could possibly get any worse even if I did."

The look of adoration that met my eyes when he pulled the blanket down made me feel bad for my pity party. It wasn't Drake's fault that things were going to hell with this wedding.

"Do you trust me?" he asked.

"Of course I do," I replied.

As soon as I answered, Drake lifted me in his arms, blankets and all. "Then let's get moving. I have a surprise for you."

There were two black stretch limos in the driveway that were being loaded up with luggage. Aubrey and her parents were helping put their stuff into one while Drake's dad and mine were loading up the other. Drea waved to me from the back seat of the car as her mom followed her inside.

"What's going on?" I asked, confused by the sight in front of me.

"I'm kidnapping you."

"Are things so bad that we're eloping?" I half-joked, not expecting the worried look that entered his eyes. "Ohmigod,

Drake. Seriously. We can't do that. We have guests coming. Flowers and food and the baker. As much as I'd love for us to run off and get married without a care in the world, it's just not possible."

"Trust me," he requested, his eyes locked with mine. "I know what I'm doing here."

"And even if he didn't, I do," his mom piped in. "Now, you two get in this car and talk for a bit. We'll ride in the other so you have some privacy."

I watched as she practically dragged our dads to the other limo before Drake climbed in ours and sat down with me on his lap.

"What the hell?" I snapped at him. "I don't understand what's going on."

"You went to bed crying last night, Alexa. That's not acceptable to me. Ever. And certainly not two days before our wedding."

"Drake," I sighed. "I know you hate seeing me cry, but things were just crazy yesterday. And I've been under so much stress lately that it was almost a relief to let some of it out with a good cry."

"Nothing about what happened last night was good, baby," he disagreed. "But today's a new day, and I'm hoping you agree with what I've decided to do."

"What did you decide?" I asked, scared to hear his answer because I wasn't sure about the gleam in his eye. He looked worried about my reaction, so I knew it had to be something big.

"We're headed to the airport. Your dad called ahead to make sure the plane would be fueled up and ready to go so he could fly us back to your hometown. When we get there, you and I are going to Town Hall to apply for a marriage license. Luckily, there's no wait and no blood tests are needed in Ohio," he started.

"But we already have a marriage license," I interrupted.

"Yeah, for here we do, but we're not going to get married here. We're going to do it there," he told me.

47

I sat up straight and bumped my head on the roof of the car. Rubbing it, I looked at him in a daze. "What did you just say?"

"Baby, please let me tell you all of it. And then, if you think it's a horrible idea, you can yell and scream at me all you want, okay?" he asked.

I nodded my head in response before he continued.

"I've been telling you that this wedding is about you and me and nobody else, but, baby, it's really about you. As long as you're happy, then I'm happy. And the only way I can see to make that happen is if we get on your dad's plane so he can take us where we should have planned to have our wedding in the first place. Where we would have planned it if I'd been paying closer attention to what you needed."

"No—" I argued, but I didn't get far because he placed his finger over my lips. I hated the idea he felt like he'd let me down when I was the one who'd agreed to get married at his parents' place when his mom had offered.

"It doesn't matter how we got to where we are today. What matters is this is easy to fix. We're going to get married in a place where the people who are most important to both of us will be there. And then, after I've made you my wife, we'll celebrate with the huge party my mom planned for us. The best of both worlds with a short two-hour flight in between," he told me.

I was stunned silent for a moment as I realized what he and everyone else must have been up to last night in order to make this work. And then I felt a huge sense of relief.

"You really did all of this for me?"

"I'd do anything for you. You have to know that by now," he said.

"And your mom isn't mad about the change in plans? Everyone's okay with this?" I didn't want her to think I didn't appreciate everything she'd already done for us so we'd have the perfect wedding, but the picture of Drake and me standing in the little gazebo and exchanging our vows where Aubrey and I used to play pretend wedding brought happy tears to my eyes.

"She was a little freaked out at first when I talked to her last night, but she's fine now. She's been on the phone and Internet making sure we'd have everything we need for tomorrow."

"But I don't even have my dress," I realized out loud.

"Taken care of," he assured me.

"Or the flowers."

"Aubrey's mom called up the local florist and sent her pictures of what you wanted. She assured her that she'd be able to duplicate what the florist here is going to do. You'll just end up with two bouquets instead of one," he explained.

"My shoes, makeup, lingerie…" I rattled off a list of things I'd need if I really was going to be a bride in a whole other city tomorrow morning.

"All packed up and ready to go. Aubrey gave me a list and double-checked to make sure I had everything you'd need."

"We're really going to do this?" I asked in wonder.

"As long as it's what you want," he replied. "You ready to fly away with me and elope, but with our families surrounding us?"

"Abso-freaking-lutely!" I squealed.

<hr />

Drake hadn't been joking when he'd told me that they had thought of everything. The next twenty-four hours flew by in a happy whirlwind. I woke up the next morning in my childhood bedroom with the man who would soon be my husband by my side. He'd put his foot down when Aubrey had said that we'd needed to spend the night apart. He'd told her that there was no way in hell that was going to happen and carted me off to my room for the night while she and his mom laughed their asses off.

We were on our way to Aubrey's house now. Although they let him get away with disappearing with me last night, we'd already gotten texts and calls asking when I was going to be at Aubrey's house this morning.

"Hey, did you forget where Aubrey lives that quickly?" I asked when he turned down the wrong street.

"Nope. We need to make a quick detour," he answered.

After a couple of turns, I realized where he was taking me. I could barely see him through the tears welling in my eyes. "The cemetery?"

"Yeah," he admitted as we turned into the parking lot.

He pulled into the spot closest to her grave and turned to me after shutting off the engine. Then he reached behind my seat and grabbed a bouquet of flowers. Red roses and white lilies—the same flowers I'd be carrying later in the day.

"For my mom?" I asked.

"I thought you might want her to be part of our day," he explained.

"Oh, God," I gasped as I threw myself across the seat and into his arms. "Yes, I do."

"C'mon," he urged.

We climbed out of the car and walked hand in hand to her plot. Drake stood waiting behind me as I took those last steps to reach her grave. I reached out to sweep some leaves off her headstone.

Marie Anne Hewett
1967 – 1992
Who knew that angels lived amongst us?
Let alone in our homes?
Beloved wife and mother.

"Hey, Mom," I whispered softly as I laid the flowers on the grass. "It's my wedding day. I'm marrying the most amazing man today. I think you'd love him as much as I do. Daddy even approves."

The wind blew gently against me and I imagined that it was her letting me know that she approved. So I told her all about how we'd met and our plans for the wedding.

"I'm sorry, baby, but we need to go," Drake came up behind me and whispered into my ear as he grasped my shoulders.

"Okay," I agreed. "I'm ready."

And I was ready. Drake had given me exactly what I'd needed today with this stop. A moment to feel connected to the mother I'd never gotten the chance to know on the most important day of my life. As we walked back to the car, I felt lighter than I had in months. It made the entire trip back home worthwhile.

❦

I stood staring at myself in the mirror in Aubrey's room. Aubrey and her mom had made sure I'd gotten into my dress without messing up my hair or makeup, but then I'd asked for a moment alone before my dad came to get me for the ceremony. My dress looked even better than it had with the new cap sleeves, and I felt like a fairy princess. When I heard the music begin playing from outside, I knew it was just about time. Then there was a soft knock on the door before my dad peeked in the room.

"You ready to go, sweetie?" he asked.

I turned to face him and he stopped walking as he stared at me in awe.

"My baby girl is all grown up. You look beautiful."

"Thanks, Daddy."

"I know between Drake and Aubrey you already have something new, something borrowed, and something blue covered. They left something old to me," my dad explained before pulling a jewelry box out of his tuxedo jacket pocket.

Aubrey had assured me that they hadn't forgotten the something old earlier in the day when I had worried it was missing. Drake had taken care of the something new with a set of teardrop diamond earrings and something borrowed with a fabulous diamond necklace that his mom had asked me to wear

51

today. Aubrey had gone the traditional route with my pastel-blue garter.

"The day I married your mom was one of the two happiest of my life, and she walked down the aisle with this wrapped around her wrist," my dad continued.

My hand trembled as I reached down to touch the simple gold bracelet he revealed when he opened the box. Knowing my mom had worn it on her wedding day made the bracelet priceless to me. I traced along the rope of gold with my fingertip.

"Your mom would be so proud of you, sweetie," he said as he pulled the bracelet out of the box and clasped it onto my wrist. "You've turned into such an amazing woman. Every time I look at you, you remind me so much of her."

"Oh, Daddy," I sighed as I felt the tears well in my eyes, threatening to drip down my cheeks and ruin my makeup.

"It's not just your looks. You have her heart too," he continued. "You were always so open and trusting. Willing to bend over backwards for other people. Until you weren't anymore because your trust had been shattered. For years, I worried that I'd never see that side of you again. Then it was like you started to come back to life when you were near Drake, and I hoped it meant what I thought it did. That you'd met the person you were meant to be with—the one who'd protect your heart the way I protected your mom's for the time I was lucky enough to have with her."

I threw myself into his arms, feeling the loss of my mom more on this day than I ever had before. "I never got to know her, yet I miss her so much, Daddy."

"I miss her too," he admitted, and in loving Drake, I finally understood how acutely he must feel her loss. "But she's always with me in my heart, and she gave me the most precious gift in the world—you. Now let's do her proud and get you down the aisle, where Drake is waiting for you."

CHAPTER 7

Drake

The moment Alexa stepped out the door on her father's arm, I had to stop myself from walking towards her. She'd always looked beautiful to me, but today, she took my breath away. Everyone around me fell away as my focus centered on her as she glided down the aisle towards me. I heard the preacher in the background before he father said that he was proudly giving her away to me today. I knew he turned and walked to his sit, but I still couldn't tear my eyes away from hers. Time felt suspended until Alexa giggled up at me when my childhood friend, who was serving as my best man, nudged me in the ribs.

I turned to look at the preacher as he cleared his throat.

"I understand the bride and groom wrote their own vows," he prompted me.

"Yes, we did," Alexa answered. "But it seems my groom might have forgotten his."

"Not for a minute," I assured her before taking a deep breath. "Alexa, the feeling that hit me the moment we first made eye contact… It was so immediate and powerful—far deeper than anything I had ever expected to feel for anyone. I had no idea what to expect, and then you opened your heart to me and showed me what love truly means. I vow to have the patience that love demands, to speak when words are needed, and to share in the silence when they are not. And to protect and cherish your heart always."

Alexa needed no reminder to begin her vows even with tears rolling down her cheeks. She gripped my fingers more firmly as she began. "Drake, you know me better than anyone else in this world, and somehow, you still manage to love me. You are my one true love, and there's a part of me today that cannot believe that I'm the lucky one who gets to marry you. I see these vows not as promises, but as privileges. I get to laugh with you and cry with you although I know you'll do everything you can to stop my tears. I get to walk with you, run with you and even fly with you. More importantly, I get to build a life with you and live with you until my dying breath many, many years from now."

I couldn't help myself as I leaned down to kiss her beautiful lips. The love shining from her eyes combined with her heartfelt words made it impossible. I brushed the tears from her cheeks with my thumbs as I reluctantly pulled away from her mouth.

"Ahem," the preacher cleared his throat to get my attention again. "The wedding ring is the outward and visible sign of an inward and spiritual grace, signifying to all the uniting of this man and this woman in holy matrimony. Dear Lord, bless the giving of these rings, that they who wear them may abide in thy peace and continue in thy favor."

When he handed me Alexa's ring, I slid it on her finger, repeating my pledge after him. "In token and pledge of our constant faith and abiding love, with this ring, I thee wed."

Then he handed Alexa my ring and she did the same before he joined our hands together. "Forasmuch as Drake and Alexa have consented together in holy wedlock and have witnessed the same before God and this company, and thereto have pledged their faith each to the other and have declared the same by joining hands and by giving and receiving rings, I pronounce that they are husband and wife together. Those whom God hath joined together let no one put asunder. Amen."

And just like that, we were finally married. My wait was over and Alexa was now my wife.

The one disadvantage to my plan for us to wed in her hometown and then fly back to mine for the reception was we barely had any time to enjoy ourselves until the night was over. We said our goodbyes to Jackson, Kaylie, and his parents, who decided to stay behind before the rest of us went to the airport. The two-hour flight flew by, as Aubrey had arranged for the photographer to come with and had her snap a million pictures en route. Before I knew it, we were back at my parents' house enjoying the reception with all of our family and friends.

Once the night was over and we were able to leave, it was straight back to the airport for us. I wanted to spend my first morning with my new bride on our honeymoon, just the two of us. The flight was less than three hours, and I had plans for that time, too. I made sure her dad wasn't the one in the pilot's seat since that would have been incredibly awkward, and once we were in the air, the pilot knew I wanted absolute privacy.

"Are you ever going to tell me where you're taking me?" Alexa asked before taking a sip of the champagne I'd just poured for her.

"I told you already. We're going to Paradise," I said.

"Yeah, but paradise could be anywhere. C'mon. Give me a hint," she pleaded.

I laughed lightly, pleased that she hadn't figured out my little joke in the last month since she'd gotten me to admit that much. "I really am taking you to Paradise, Alexa. Paradise Island in the Bahamas. To the most amazing hotel I could find with a private villa just for the two of us. White sand beaches, romantic gardens, tennis courts, and a golf course."

"Are we staying long enough to enjoy all that?"

"Did I mention they have amazing room service, too? Since, odds are, we'll barely leave the room even though we're going to be there for a whole week," I teased.

"Room service and you? Sounds like the perfect honeymoon to me," she said. "But golf and tennis are out since you only told me to pack lingerie and bikinis."

"See, you married a brilliant man. He has the best ideas," I replied. "In fact, he's about to show you one of his better ones right now."

"Oh he is, is he?"

I lifted the glass out of her hand and set it down. Pulling her into my lap, I whispered my idea into her ear. "How about you and I finally join the mile high club together?"

"Seriously?" she gasped.

"It's just you, me, and the pilot. Nobody to bother us back here, and I suggested he take a page from your book and put on some noise-canceling headphones for the flight," I explained. "Seems fitting to me now that I have the brains behind the mile high club charter flights in the back of the plane all to myself that I take full advantage of the opportunity."

"Yes," she whispered, leaning down to place a kiss against my lips. "I've always wondered what it would be like to do my favorite thing in the world in my favorite place in the world."

"Your wish is my command, baby. All you ever have to do is ask," I told her before smashing my mouth against hers

I tugged on her bottom lip down with my teeth, making her gasp. My tongue dove inside as soon as her lips parted, mimicking what my cock was going to do to her pussy soon. Clenching her hair in my hands, I held her in place so I could devour her mouth. Once we were both gasping for air, I cupped her ass and pulled her over me so her pussy was resting right over my cock. Feeling her wet heat through her dress, I couldn't stop myself from grinding my hips against her.

"Please, Drake. Make love to me, my husband," she begged.

"Fuck," I groaned as I swiftly unzipped the front of my pants to open them.

As soon as I got them open, my cock sprang free—fully erect and throbbing in need. When Alexa lifted the hem of her dress, the sight of her white-lace-clad pussy made my mouth water. I couldn't resist pulling her body up as my head dipped low so I could get a little taste first.

Running my tongue over the damp material, I inhaled the scent of her arousal as it drifted up to me before I ripped the panties off her body and drove my tongue inside. She was dripping wet and tasted amazing. I held her ass in one hand while she balanced herself on her knees and held on to the back of the seat. Flicking my tongue over her clit, I pumped two fingers inside until she came.

"Drake," she moaned as her pussy fluttered against me while she trembled in my arms.

As soon as her climax ended, I pulled her down and slid up inside her wet pussy. Buried deep, I felt her walls grip me tight as I savored the feel of her wrapped around me.

"Baby, this isn't gonna last very long. I need to move," I moaned.

I felt another flutter as she heard me, and she began to move too, rotating her hips in circles at the end of each of my thrusts. I hammered into her, so deep that my cock was nudging her cervix. Wanting her to go with me, I released her hip and started to rub her clit with my thumb. The added stimulation was just enough, and she came for me again.

I continued to pound into her, holding her hips in place now so she couldn't move.

"So fucking tight like this," I groaned. Our eyes were locked together, so I could tell when she came back to her senses.

"I love you," she whispered. "My husband."

Her words were my undoing. "My wife. Fuck," I grunted as I emptied myself inside her. "Love you too, baby," I whispered as I captured her lips with mine, happy that Alexa was finally my wife – mind, body, and soul.

EPILOGUE

Alexa
Three Years Later

Gazing down into my son's eyes for the very first time, I couldn't help but wonder why I'd ever resisted the idea of having a baby in the first place. My honorary niece was born the day we'd returned from our honeymoon, and that had been the start of the baby bug for me. I had still been scared about having one, but Kaylie and Jackson had made it look easy with Kassidy. Kaylie was released from bed rest as soon as she hit the thirty-six-week mark and went into labor a couple of days later. After all the worrying of the weeks before, Kassidy's birth was one of the quickest for a first-time mom her doctor had ever seen.

We had to wait for a little while though because Drake's years of hard training paid off when his rugby team made it into the Olympics during the Final Olympic Qualification Tournament. It was literally their last chance since they hadn't made it through the Sevens World Series or the Regional Association Sevens Championships.

I was incredibly blessed to have the opportunity to stay by his side throughout it all, and a pregnancy wouldn't have allowed me to travel safely. After working hard for so many years, I thought I would miss my time in the pilot's seat, but he made sure I got plenty of time to fly even if it was usually just the two of us or him and some of the guys from the team. Being a pilot had come in handy many times over the years, allowing us the opportunity to see family and friends no matter how hard his schedule was.

Although the team didn't win the gold, they did earn a bronze medal. An accomplishment we celebrated with the decision to start the next chapter of our life—one that included children. I got off the pill, and less than six months later, there was a plus sign on the pregnancy test Drake had insisted I use when I was being super cranky with him one morning. Staring down at it in my hand, I was struck by the fear that I would share the same fate as my mom when she had given birth to me. But all the worry that had lived inside me for the last eight and a half months was erased the moment I saw him looking up at me so trustingly.

"I'm so proud of you," Drake whispered in awe. "Look what you did. He's so perfect."

He was a replica of his dad. The two men in my life who owned my heart.

"He really is. I can't believe he's finally here. Our little Tanner Jacob."

❦

Five more years later...

"Mommy!" Aubrey's daughter, Veronika, ran up to us, blond pigtails flying behind and her face red from the exertion of playing with all the other kids. "Tanner isn't really my cousin like Kassidy and Kennedy are, right?"

"No, baby. Auntie Lexi isn't really Mommy's sister, so Tanner isn't really your cousin, but he's just like family," she answered.

"Good," Veronika said with a satisfied grin on her face. "'Cause when I grow up, I'm gonna marry him," she finished before racing off again.

"I think I've finally decided to forgive Drake for stealing away the chance I had of you and me becoming sisters when he swept you off your feet back in college," Aubrey told me.

60

"Yeah, 'cause now we might have the chance to be something even better together—grandmothers," I replied as we watched Veronika chase after Tanner.

"If not with those two, then maybe the next round," she said as she touched her flat stomach. She and Luka just found out a week ago that they were expecting again.

"Only if you get the boy this time," I answered, rubbing my rounded belly. We were expecting a girl this time—one we were going to name in loving memory of my mom. Marie Anne Bennett.

ACKNOWLEDGMENTS

My boys – Thank you for not complaining too much about the piles of laundry & carry-out meals while I was writing. Yes, I know… yet again. I love you!

Mom – Thank you for always supporting me and inspiring me to live my dream.

Yolanda – Thanks for being a great friend. Even though we live states away from each other, your continued support means the world to me.

Mickey – I am so grateful to have found an editor like you! Thanks for putting your mad editing skills to good use for me. This book seriously wouldn't have released on time if you weren't so amazing!

Melissa – Thank you so much for the wonderful cover! It's such a beautiful way to end the series.

Panty dropping Book Blog – Thanks for your help getting the word out about my books. Heather has been great and you all have done an amazing job pimping me! The bloggers that work with you have been so generous with their time and efforts on my behalf.

FBGM girls – You know who you are and you damn well know why I love you so much! For reals.

Readers/Bloggers – Thank you from the bottom of my heart for taking a chance on me. I would not be living my dream right now if it weren't for all of you.

ABOUT THE AUTHOR

I absolutely adore reading—always have and always will. When I was growing up, my friends used to tease me when I would trail after them, trying to read and walk at the same time. If I have downtime, odds are you will find me reading or writing.

I am the mother of two wonderful sons who have inspired me to chase my dream of being an author. I want them to learn from me that you can live your dream as long as you are willing to work for it.

When I told my mom that my new year's resolution was to self-publish a book in 2013, she pretty much told me, "About time!"

Connect with me online!

Facebook: http://www.facebook.com/rochellepaigeauthor

Twitter: @rochellepaige1

Goodreads:
https://www.goodreads.com/author/show/7328358.Rochelle_Paige

Website: http://www.rochellepaige.com

SUCKED INTO LOVE
BACHELORETTE PARTY BOOK 1
BLYTHE COLLEGE SPIN-OFF SERIES
AVAILABLE NOW

No woman ever expects to meet the man of her dreams at her bachelorette party...

It's just Jocelyn's luck that she meets her match at the fake bachelorette party her best friend throws for her. She knows better than to get pulled into any of Cee-Cee's antics. It must have been sheer exhaustion that made her agree to help her best friend out with a work project - one that ended up with her playing bachelorette for the night!

No man ever wants to be knocked off his feet by a woman he meets while she's wearing a bachelorette "suck for a buck" shirt...

Andrew knows that he wants Jocelyn the moment he lays eyes on her, but he's never been one to poach on another man's territory. He walks away but finds himself changed by the experience. Imagine his surprise when he sees her again, only to discover she isn't married and has never even been engaged.

AND COMING SOON...
CHECKED INTO LOVE
BACHELORETTE PARTY BOOK 1

Made in the USA
Lexington, KY
10 November 2014